Escaping the Storm

PRAISE FOR *STORYSHARES*

"One of the brightest innovators and game-changers in the education industry."
– Forbes

"Your success in applying research-validated practices to promote literacy serves as a valuable model for other organizations seeking to create evidence-based literacy programs."

- Library of Congress

"We need powerful social and educational innovation, and Storyshares is breaking new ground. The organization addresses critical problems facing our students and teachers. I am excited about the strategies it brings to the collective work of making sure every student has an equal chance in life."
– Teach For America

"Around the world, this is one of the up-and-coming trailblazers changing the landscape of literacy and education."
- International Literacy Association

"It's the perfect idea. There's really nothing like this. I mean wow, this will be a wonderful experience for young people."   - Andrea Davis Pinkney, Executive Director, Scholastic

"Reading for meaning opens opportunities for a lifetime of learning. Providing emerging readers with engaging texts that are designed to offer both challenges and support for each individual will improve their lives for years to come. Storyshares is a wonderful start."
- David Rose, Co-founder of CAST & UDL

Escaping the Storm

Katrina Wong

STORYSHARES

Story Share, Inc.
New York. Boston. Philadelphia

Storyshares
Story Share, Inc.
24 N. Bryn Mawr Avenue #340
Bryn Mawr, PA 19010-3304
www.storyshares.org

Inspiring reading with a new kind of book.

Interest Level: Middle School
Grade Level Equivalent: 2.8

9781642611496

Book design by Storyshares

Printed in the United States of America

Storyshares Presents

1

Naomi

It's dark.

It's death.

It's war.

I awoke to a sound. The same sound that played in my head every so often: screams. The German soldiers were taking another, just like they took Chrissy.

It wasn't unusual for them to show up at doorsteps and drag people away. When they came for you, you were to suffer an inevitable fate. No one was quite sure what happened once you were taken, and I didn't plan on finding out.

Today was the day I would disappear forever. I didn't know where I was headed. Anywhere was better than here. They'd come for me like they came for Chrissy.

After all, we were Jewish.

2

Blaze

It's fierce.

It's power.

It's war.

They screamed. They always screamed. Why were they so afraid? We were saving our people. They were nothing but a poisonous race that must be exterminated.

Their thoughts, feelings, and importance were nothing compared to us. We dragged the woman and her daughter from the property.

They tried to reach for each other; we pulled them away.

Heil Hitler!

3

Michaela

It's ignorant.

It's stupid.

It's war.

I was on my way home when I saw it. Those bastards were taking Abbey and her mother. To where? I did not know. I just knew it wasn't good.

"Stop!" I pleaded. I ran over to the scene. He pushed me away. His hands gripped tightly around my arms, allowing little movement.

"Stand back," he said sharply. "This doesn't concern you."

I could kill him. I wanted to kill him. I wanted to wrap my hands around his throat until there was no life left.

I snapped out of it. "She's German!" I shouted. "She's German, dammit!" I'd say anything to get them to stop. I'd lie and holler, but they wouldn't listen.

The soldier didn't let go of me until Abbey was locked away in the truck.

"She's dirty," he whispered. "We did you a favor."

I hated this war. I hated my country.

4

Naomi

I walked through the forest. I never looked back. Would anyone notice? Would anyone care? They wouldn't.

Naomi Cohen died nearly a year ago, when my sister was taken. Chrissy.

The thought of her made me twitch. I wanted to forget. I could forget, couldn't I?

No. I couldn't.

I remember that day like it happened yesterday. It started off clear and sunny. It seemed as if nothing could go wrong, except everything did. We were beginning to make lunch. I was happy. Happy about what? I could not remember.

There was a knock at the door, a knock that would haunt me for the rest of my life. My mother answered it. Soldiers stood before us.

"Your daughter, Christine Cohen, failed to respond to the order sent by the Gestapo on July 10 of 1942," the soldier stated with little emotion, if any at all.

The calling. How could I forget about the calling? Perhaps I wanted so desperately for it not to be true, that I managed to fool myself.

"What order?" my mother asked. "We didn't receive an order." Her lying was a bad idea, but what other ideas were there? They were going to take Chrissy, and no one could stop them.

"I hid the papers from my family in hopes I wouldn't have to leave them," my sister said suddenly.

Everyone turned to her.

"I'm sorry. It was a stupid idea."

"A stupid idea indeed," one of the soldiers said. I crossed my arms so they wouldn't notice my hands shaking. What would they do to her? What would they do to me?

All three of them had guns in their pockets. For a short moment I actually believed they would kill us. But dying by gunfire was probably one of the best ways to die these days.

They wouldn't do that.

"Arrest her," one ordered. They would just take Chrissy. Were we not all considered criminals in their eyes?

"No!" my mother screeched. It was a screech like none other. She yanked the soldier's arm away from my sister. Stupid.

They shot her. No words. No emotion. Just gunfire. My father and I stood there, jaws dropped. I watched as they loaded Chrissy into the truck. She was crying. She knew her fate. She knew her doom.

That was the last time I saw her.

Escaping the Storm

5

Blaze

The Jews. The Polish. The weak. They were all considered worthless. The only pure people in the world were the Germans.

I arrested a young girl today, my first arrest. I was almost sure she attended my school a couple years ago. I couldn't quite remember. I had left the academy at sixteen, when I was drafted to become a soldier. That was only two years ago, but it seemed like so much longer.

It wasn't until I joined that I realized the truth. Everyone's fate was sealed from the moment they were born. And only the Germans would survive this war.

I didn't like the arrests. Nazis claimed these people to be dirty. I didn't see it. They must be really good at hiding it.

Heil Hitler!

6

Michaela

Why did we do this? What had we become? People followed blindly. I couldn't. Not after what I'd seen them do to half of my school, half of my country.

My family wouldn't listen. They too followed blindly. I had to leave. I no longer belonged in the place I once called home.

The Germans had become murderers.

We weren't what we claimed to be. Nobody saw it. I was alone. Would I be alone forever? Alone was better than here. How could I stay? After what we've done? After what I haven't done?

The war had just begun.

There was more to come.

No one could save us.

Not anymore.

7

Naomi

Father and I left early in the morning. We put on four layers of clothes, and the few items we decided to bring with us were squished into a single handbag. If anyone on the streets suspected us of fleeing, we would be charged as criminals and then taken.

Father said we were heading to Switzerland. Thousands of other Jews had supposedly fled there at the beginning of the war. It was uncertain if those rumors were true or not, but it was our only chance. And it was a chance we were willing to take.

I didn't know how I would like Switzerland. We had family there, but we never talked to them. I figured that would soon change.

The forest was cold. It was the winter of 1943. It had been four years since the war began.

How much longer could this go on? Perhaps it would continue for eternity.

We continued to walk through the forest. The roads were reserved for the military. It wasn't safe for us to be out in the open. My feet began to ache.

I found myself constantly asking the question, "How much farther to Switzerland?"

Father always had the same answer. "Too far," he'd say. I wasn't sure I could take much more of this.

Minutes felt like hours, and hours felt like days. I kept reminding myself that this was necessary. It would be worth it. If I gave up now, I'd die. Father stopped ahead.

"What is it?" I asked. "What's wrong?"

It was a dumb question; a million things were wrong.

He didn't reply. I walked over to him.

When I got close enough, he finally told me not to look. I looked anyway. Curiosity always got the best of me.

There were bodies. Frozen bodies, most of them children. How did they die? Did it matter? It mattered to me.

There was blood stained on a woman's coat. Children laid motionless next to her. Was the woman shot? Had her children stayed with her until the cold became too much to bear? There were many possibilities, but that one seemed most likely.

"We need to keep going," Father ordered. "Whoever did that could still be near. We need to stay quiet."

I didn't let it show, but those words terrified me. I knew it terrified him too, so I tried to be brave. Every step was a ticking time bomb. Stepping on a twig could cost us our lives. I carefully watched everywhere I placed my feet, but it didn't matter.

When I looked up, I saw a soldier, and his gun was pointed at me.

8

Blaze

We received news early this morning that the Soviets were sending an army towards Germany. Those Russian soldiers were idioten. A small army against the Germans? They stood no chance.

I was one of the many men assigned to defeat them. We were to take a path through the woods; they wouldn't see us that way.

I sometimes found it strange how just two years ago I was attending school. Back when my biggest struggle was trying to get a girl to notice me.

How much my life had changed.

When I joined the military, I was fearful I would be the youngest one there. I wasn't. Despite officially having to be eighteen, there were kids as young as fourteen who had joined.

I thought long and hard about why someone would want to join war at such a young age, but then I realized I myself was only sixteen. It wasn't that I wanted to fight. I hated fighting. But I couldn't just stand back and watch.

Still, I often wondered what I was fighting for. Was I the only one who couldn't seem to hate the Jews, or the Polish, or anyone else?

No matter how hard I tried?

When I looked at them I saw myself. I had only made one arrest, and yet it was enough for me to never want to make another. I stopped myself. I couldn't have these thoughts. The Jews, the Polish, the weak. They were all worthless.

Yes. That was right. Worthless.

By nightfall, we were deep into the forest. It was almost peaceful. We weren't exactly sure how close the Soviets were, but we had a pretty good estimate. We would come across them in another hour or so.

I had been a part of this war for two years now. Up until last week, however, I had done nothing more than check people's papers as they attempted to cross the border into Germany.

I guess my fear was visible, because as we walked a soldier said to me, "Fear not, sir. The Russians are nothing. They have their numbers, but our numbers are bigger."

He was an old man. I assumed he had experience. His hair was white and he appeared as if he ate a little too much.

"Right," I agreed, "I shouldn't be worrying." But truth was; I wasn't afraid of what they'd do to us. I was afraid of what we'd do to them.

Hours passed; there was still no sign of the Russians. Were we sure we were in the right place?

Bang.

Everyone turned, debating whether or not to find out what that was.

"I'll go," I stated. No one else was going to do it, and I had a feeling finding out was a safer option than staying here. I walked swiftly through the trees, following the cries of a young girl. When I got there, there was a soldier holding his gun against a girl's forehead.

Next to her was an old man, dead. I assumed he was her father. The soldier was one of us; he was German. The girl must be Jewish, maybe Polish.

I looked to the soldier, then to the girl.

I grabbed my gun and fired.

Heil Hitler.

9

Michaela

I left home as soon as the sun rose. I told my parents I was going to my friend's house to study. When they realized I wasn't coming home, would they care? I hoped they would, but I hadn't seen eye to eye with them in over four years.

I was a nuisance to them. They wouldn't care. They would hardly even notice.

I walked through the woods alone. It was so cold. The wind blew right through my coat, sending chills throughout my body. I tried to move my fingers, but they were numb. I placed them in my pockets.

By the time it was noon, I had been walking for hours. My stomach pained from hunger, and my legs begged me to stop.

I sat against a tree. I rested for a few minutes. I had a few minutes, right? Those minutes became hours. Every time I stood up my feet ordered me to sit down.

The hunger worsened. I brought food with me, but I needed to save it. Food was scarce these days, even before I left. Everyone received rations, and because I was German, I received more than most. I didn't take much with me, however, because it would appear suspicious. Nobody brings week's worth of food with them to a study session.

When night fell, I finally brought myself to stand up. I needed to move. The forest was the worst place to be at night. It lurked with soldiers. It was only a few moments later when I heard footsteps. Someone was following me. A million thoughts crowded my mind. Who were they? What did they want? Were they going to kill me? I had no weapon to protect myself with. I was on my own.

My heart pounded faster than I ever thought it could. I feared if it went any faster it would explode. I turned. I could feel my pulse in my hands. Was this the end? I had survived four years of the war. That was more than most. I let out a long sigh. It wasn't until I released them that I noticed my nails were digging into my palms.

A young boy stood before me. What had he been through? What had he seen? "Mother," he said. Did he think I was his mother? "Help. Please." He wanted me to help his mother?

I started to walk away. I didn't trust him. I couldn't trust anyone, not even a kid. He pleaded for me to stop, but his cries soon became silent. I turned around and he was gone.

I had either just saved myself, or killed someone else. Perhaps both.

Escaping the Storm

10

Naomi

The gun felt cold against my forehead. He killed Father. Why did this always happen? Why did people always have to die? I closed my eyes tightly. My tears felt like glue. I accepted my fate. The gun went off.

I felt nothing. Was I dead? I opened my eyes. The soldier was motionless on the ground, blood pouring from the hole between his eyes. Another soldier began to walk towards me. He was German also. Did he know who I was?

Did he know what I was? He couldn't have known I was Jewish. He wouldn't have saved me.

"You're welcome," he said.

I did not reply.

"No response?" His words grew angry. "No wonder we hate you Jews. You're downright stupid." He knew. He had saved me. Now he would kill me.

He was German; I was Jewish. This could only end so many ways. Why save me? It didn't make sense. Perhaps he wanted the pleasure all to himself.

"Never speak of this," he said. "Or I will kill you."

What? Was I wrong about him? He couldn't be German. A German would've killed me already. It was undeniable though; he was German. He began to walk away; I followed.

"You're not going to kill me," I said. "You would've done it already."

"Never too late."

I walked with him only a few feet before he stopped and turned to me.

"Don't follow me." His words were sharp and clear.

"Who are you?" I wondered.

"No one. Just go."

"I won't make it alone. I need to get to Switzerland, please!" It was no use. He wasn't going to stop. "Okay," I sighed. "Thank you for giving me a chance."

Escaping the Storm

11

Blaze

"Thank you for giving me a chance," she said. I shouldn't have saved her. I shouldn't have given her that chance. She was dirty. Yes. Of course she was dirty. She was a Jew.

I kept walking. If I never mentioned it, it never happened, right? I didn't have time to think about it. I needed to get back to my group; they must've come across the Russians by now.

I traced my steps, walked the exact same way I came. They were gone. Where could they be? They couldn't have gone far. If I started now, I could catch up to them by daylight. But did I really want to go back?

Yes. Of course I wanted to go back. It was my duty.

I thought of the Jewish girl. She'd die without me. I told myself she deserved it. Of course she deserved it.

Switzerland. She wouldn't make it. Who have I become? I knew what I needed to do.

Heil Hitler.

12

Michaela

It was warm in here. The house was deserted. There was a half-eaten chocolate cake on the kitchen table; mold grew on it. Someone had a really schrecklich birthday.

I raided the kitchen; all I found was a can of beans. I banged it against the counter until it cracked open. There weren't any forks. I didn't care. I scooped the beans out with my fingers and shoved them into my mouth. The taste was disgusting, but ever so satisfying. What had the world come to? What had my country become?

In a few years, would people believe me when I told them it wasn't always this way? Germany used to be the birthplace of peace. My home. Now it was nothing but a black hole of death.

I didn't want to leave that boy out on the road. His mother must be dead by now, if there was a mother. I hated what the war had done to me. I hated what I had become. His cries played in my head over and over. Should I have helped him? What could I have done? I could have done everything.

I didn't have time to feel remorse. It would be daylight soon, and I still had no idea where I was going. France, Poland, Belgium, the Netherlands. They were all taken. What country was left? I wasn't sure there were any. If only I could get to America. America. The one place they hadn't gotten to.

Getting there was virtually impossible. Ships would be crowded with German soldiers. Too many questions would be asked. America was my lost dream. I placed the empty can of beans on the table. It left a nasty taste it my mouth, and I had no toothbrush to brush it away. I drank the last sip of my water.

There was none left. What would I do now? That was

tomorrow's problem. I threw myself onto the couch. I snuggled under my coat and closed my eyes. It wasn't until then I realized how tired I was. I slept soundly for a while, until I was interrupted by a loud knock at the door.

A knock. Who could that be? A soldier? The boy? This could be the end of Michaela Muller. And yet, all I could think was that a can of beans may have been my last meal.

13

Naomi

The German soldier was gone. My family was gone. My friends must be dead. I was alone. I could go after him. I could beg him to help me. Would he? He already had. It began to snow. It was a beautiful sight, the snow landing perfectly on the trees and falling ever so delicately to the soil.

I turned to show Father. Of course, he wasn't there.

I walked deeper into the forest. I didn't realize how deep until there was no forest left. What was I supposed to do now? The forest was my life vest; was there a point to wearing a life vest if I would drown anyway?

I left the trees, walking along the side of the road. If I were discovered I would be killed. Could I be killed if I was already dead? Anything seemed possible these days. I walked for a while and then I heard something.

Footsteps. The German soldier had come back for me. I knew he would. I turned my head and let out a shriek. There was a boy. He was covered in blood.

"Mother," he said. He fell to the ground crying. What was I supposed to do? What had happened to his mother? Was he suffering the same fate as I was? A newly-made orphan, fleeing from a place that was once called home.

I walked slowly over to him. I didn't want to scare him away. "Are you okay?" I asked. Dumb question.

He shook his head.

"It's alright," I whispered. "I'll help you." I picked the boy up; he rested his head against my chest. What had this boy seen? What had he done? We'd all done something, some worse than others. He trusted me. Could I trust him?

I couldn't carry him forever, but I wouldn't have to.

There was a small house up ahead. The lights were on; someone was home. Was it safe to knock? Certainly not. What choice did I have? We'd freeze to death out here.

A German soldier didn't kill me, a Jewish girl. I liked my odds today. I walked up the steps, my heart pounding hard. I'm sure the boy could feel it. If I was wrong about this, we would both die... but what if I was right? I had to take the chance.

I took it. I knocked.

14

Blaze

I walked back towards the Jewish girl. When I got to her, I would kill her. Yes. Of course I would kill her. She was so young; so innocent. But she was dirty, ever so dirty. She had to be, right? She was Jewish.

I swear this was the spot. Where could she have gone? Everyone kept leaving.

I looked down. Footprints. For the first time in four

years I was glad to see snow. What a stupid girl she was, leaving her footprints so visible in the snow. I followed her tracks, erasing her footprints from existence. I was doing this because her death would be my doing.

Could I kill her? I told myself I could. "You won't kill me," her words echoed. "You would've done it already." What a silly thing to say. Certainly I couldn't believe a word she said. She was Jewish.

I couldn't stop thinking about the arrest I made. What would happen to that girl and her mother? What had already happened? I snapped out of it. Whatever happened to them was their own fault. They were Jewish. They were dirty.

Her tracks ended. The forest was behind me. Great. Which way do I go? Right was always right, nein? I began to walk. I would see her soon. How would I kill her? Would I shoot her?

Yes. That was the right thing to do. I walked for what felt like forever. There was still no sign of the Jewish girl. I looked straight ahead; I had to squint to see it, but it was there. T

he house's lights were on. The Jewish girl was in there. I walked up the steps. I held my hand to my gun. What if I was wrong? What if this wasn't the Jewish girl? What would they think of me? Would they think I was a deserter? Was I a deserter? I would tell them I was following the tracks of a young Jewish girl, and they led me here.

That was the truth, wasn't it?

I knocked.

Heil Hitler.

Escaping the Storm

15

Michaela

I held my breath. My fingers trembled as they gripped the knob. I opened the door. A girl? The boy. He was covered in blood. The girl had saved him. I was glad someone had.

"Please," she begged. "Help us." I had said no before. I couldn't say it again. I opened the door wider and motioned them in. It took everything she had for her to carry the boy into the house. I could sense the relief she felt when she placed him onto the couch. The boy was asleep. He would sleep for a while.

"Thank you," she said. People had thanked me a lot in the last few years, but she was the only one, I felt, who meant it.

I didn't say anything. I just nodded. Who was this girl? How long had she been out there? Why was she alone?

"Is it just you?" I asked, closing the door.

"You didn't notice the boy?"

She seemed shocked I didn't notice a boy covered in blood.

"I came across him earlier," I explained. "I know he's not with you."

"He is now." Her voice became stern. "Why are you alone?" she questioned.

"You first." The girl sighed. She looked to the floor, her eyes growing red. Was she going to cry? I thought she would, but she didn't. "My family was murdered. It's just me." I didn't need her to say anything else. Those few words said a lot. She had suffered more than I ever would.

"I couldn't stay," I said. "Everything they're doing is

wrong. They're murderers. I'm not one of them." Her eyes lit up. I knew then she was one of the hunted. Still, I wondered, who was she? "I'm not one of them either," she claimed. We shared a smile, both of us wondering the same thing. Could the other be trusted?

It was about an hour or so later when we jolted up by the sound. There was a knock on the door. Another one. I was beginning to feel my chances were better outside in the open.

I turned to the girl. She looked terrified. "Answer it," she whispered. "They know we're here." She was right. If I didn't open the door they'd open it for me. That really would be the end of Michaela Muller. I walked to the door, my fingers trembling all over again. I twisted the knob. The door opened.

Escaping the Storm

16

Naomi

She opened the door. I knelt behind the couch. If he came inside, that was the end. She said she wasn't one of them. I desperately hoped she had meant it.

"Good morning," Michaela said. I believe that's what she said her name was. "Is there a reason for you to disturb me so early?" Her words were angry. It was clear she didn't like whoever was on the other side of that door. I couldn't see what was going on, but there was a long pause. Long enough to make me worry.

"So sorry," someone finally replied. The voice sounded strangely familiar, but I couldn't place it. "I was following the tracks of a young Jewish girl, and they led me here. Have you seen anyone who fits that description?"

I gulped. Would she sell me out?

"No," she lied. She lied for me. "Well please inform the Gestapo if you do," the man replied. He was the German soldier.

I came out from behind the couch and into the open. My new ally looked at me as I had just signed our death papers. I suppose if it had been anyone else at the door, it would've been true. The German soldier stared at me intently. His shock was clear. Why would a superior aid a fugitive? Had he realized he'd done the same?

The soldier thought he was a good German; I was glad he wasn't. The tension in the room was unbearable. Their voices said nothing, but their expressions said it for them.

Michaela was glaring at him; he kept trying to avoid eye contact with her, but was miserably failing.

"I thought you never wanted to see me again," I broke the silence. The soldier turned to me. He was keeping his hand on his gun the entire time. "Come to shoot me?" I questioned. I knew he hadn't.

He looked back at Michaela. Was I missing something? His hand released from his gun.

"Switzerland," he said. "I need to get there too."

Escaping the Storm

17

Blaze

I had never been placed in a more awkward situation in my life. I stood in a room with a girl whose friend had just been taken by me, and a girl whose life was threatened by me. The Jewish girl asked me if I came to kill her; I had, but everything inside me told me I couldn't.

I possessed a strong urge to help her. I knew I shouldn't, but the damage was already done. Why hadn't I just let that soldier kill her in the woods?

I told her I'd take her to Switzerland. She didn't seem surprised by it. Why should she be surprised, though? I was only doing this because I knew Germany was better off without her.

Heil Hitler.

18

Michaela

I didn't trust the soldier, but Naomi seemed to. I didn't understand. He took Abbey yesterday, and now he was bent on getting us to safety? It made no sense to me. Nevertheless, we could really use the help of a German soldier.

"What's your name?" I asked. "If we're going to be traveling hundreds of kilometers together, I might as well know."

He gave me a long look, deciding whether or not I was trustworthy enough for him to tell me. "Blaze," he finally said. "And yours?" Blaze. What an odd name.

"Michaela," I responded; I guess last names weren't a priority anymore.

"I'm Naomi."

The soldier and I both looked to the young Jewish girl.

"In case anyone cares."

I couldn't help but smile. It was something I hadn't done in a long time. Who would've known a sworn enemy would be the key to my happiness?

19

Naomi

The sun had finally made an appearance. Everyone was fast asleep at that point; they wanted a good rest before we traveled six hundred sixty-one kilometers to Switzerland. The boy stayed awake with me. We were both haunted by the screams of our families.

I didn't grasp the fact that my father was dead yet. His presence was the only thing that kept me going. I couldn't think about; I'd lose control. Everyone still living had lost something. How could I feel bad for myself when I knew the boy had lost so much more?

He didn't just lose his family; he lost his childhood. Hope faded a long time ago from the world, but I couldn't help but feel that a piece of it still lingered inside me.

Nothing could last forever.

Bad things always ended, as did good ones.

Even before all this.

Maybe the war would end tomorrow; maybe it'd end in a thousand years.

The important thing was to keep hold of the last piece of hope that was left, the piece that so many had abandoned.

I had one shot at life. I intended to stay living until I'd made the most of it.

20

Blaze

Six hundred sixty-one kilometers. I reckoned it'd take us ten days to get there, if we got there. We had no water, and only a limited supply of food.

My papers listed me as a low-ranked soldier; if we were found they'd label me a deserter.

Michaela's papers listed her as a wealthy German; if we were found, they'd label her a traitor.

Naomi's papers listed her as a Jew; if we were found, they'd kill her. The boy didn't have any papers. A lot could go wrong, but we didn't think about that.

"Ready to go?" Michaela asked.

"Ready as ever." Naomi replied.

I opened the door; the coldness of the air instantly filled the room. Snow remained on the ground from the previous day, and the sky was a dull grey. My body shivered, but I walked deeper into the chilled weather anyway.

We were the strangest group, thrown together by fate, but staying together by choice.

We were supposed to hate each other. I was supposed to kill Naomi, and Michaela was supposed to thank me for it. Were we the only three who saw things differently?

What would we do once we got to Switzerland?

Would we go on our separate ways and never speak of each other again? There was great tension among our group. Michaela blamed me for what happened to her friend; I blamed myself too.

Naomi tried to get the boy to talk to her, but he wouldn't have it. No one knew each other; no one trusted each other.

I guess it wouldn't matter.

If it came to it, I'd choose myself over them. We all would.

Heil Hitler.

Escaping the Storm

21

Michaela

I was almost sure I had frostbite in my toes; my fingers were bright red and every breath was visible in the air. Why was I doing this? If we were caught, would I turn against them? I hoped I wouldn't, but I couldn't help but feel that I would. That was why I didn't trust people anymore; even the nicest ones could turn against you.

All four of us walked along the endless road for hours. I looked down at the boy. Did he blame me for his mother? He was three at best. Did he even know what was going on?

"Ruhig, quiet," Naomi said suddenly. No one was talking, so I was a bit confused as to why she would say that. Regardless, everyone stopped walking.

"What?" Blaze questioned. He was just as confused as I was.

"Do you hear that?" Naomi asked. There was nothing at first, but then it came. The sound grew louder with each second. Planes. We all looked at each other hopelessly. There was nowhere to run, nowhere to hide. We were doomed. They'd find us. They'd kill us. That'd be the end of us.

But they didn't come; they did something much worse. They dropped things from the sky. We watched them fall.

Boom.

22

Naomi

Boom.

The sound was treacherous. Some trees fell, others burned. I was pulled to the ground; a body hovered over mine, holding me close. I didn't realize who it was until he shouted, "Close your eyes!" Close my eyes? Why would I need to do that?

"Oh my God!" Michaela screamed. The sound

startled me. I looked up and saw a cloud of dust heading right towards us.

"The boy!" I shouted. "Where is he?" I couldn't get up to protect him.

"I'll get him!" Michaela yelled, but it was too late. The smoke had engulfed us. Blaze's hands covered my eyes and my nose. It was difficult to breath. I heard a loud crack and knew something was about to fall. I thought it would crush us, but it didn't. It landed right next to us; I could feel the ground rumble when it fell. It wasn't until moments later when Blaze released his hands from my face that I felt the air rush into my lungs. Most of the smoke had left the area, but there was still enough there to make us all cough. The tree was inches from my face.

Blaze helped me from the ground.

I saw Michaela on the other side of the tree. She was covered in ash; we all were.

"Is everyone okay?" Blaze asked.

"Yeah," I replied.

"Is the boy with you, Michaela?" Her face turned blue. She had been staring at the tree, choking on her tears. "Not anymore," she whispered. I looked down. The tree had spared me, but the boy wasn't so lucky.

23

Blaze

Naomi and Michaela tried to pull the boy out from under the tree; it was no use. The tree was too big, and the boy was too small.

"We have to go," I said.

Naomi shot me a death stare. That girl's heart was too big.

"We can't just leave him here!" Michaela cried.

"This isn't a negotiation," I stated. "You're not going to be able to get him out from under there. He's gone. People heard that bomb; there will be squad teams here in no time searching for survivors."

It didn't take them long to realize I was right. Michaela looked from the boy to Naomi. I knew she felt responsible; she didn't get to him in time.

"Come on," Naomi said to her. "He's with his mother now."

It wouldn't be until a few days later that they would tell me about their encounter with the boy in the woods.

We took refuge in another abandoned house. It became quite frightening how many were showing up.

Michaela was fast asleep at that point; it wasn't questionable how exhausted she was.

Naomi and I sat on one of the couches. She was reading a book I found in one of the bedrooms. I was sitting there deep in thought.

"I don't think I ever thanked you," Naomi said through the silence.

"You did," I responded.

"No," she stated. "Not about that."

If not about the soldier, then what? "You protected me from the bomb," she began.

"Oh. I didn't-"

"Shut up," she told me. "I know somewhere in there is an actual heart."

I was shocked. "What makes you so sure?" I asked.

"That you care?" She laughed. She looked at me with her innocent blue eyes and said, "You know you really care about someone when you have to convince yourself you don't." Naomi turned her face away from me and back into her book.

I wanted to tell her she saved my life. I wanted her to know everything she'd done for me, but I said nothing. I would regret that decision for the rest of my life.

Hitler.

Did I still stand for what he believed in? Did I ever? I'd been told for the longest time to worship that man. I always thought I had to, but Naomi taught me differently. She was three years younger than I was, but ten years wiser.

The young Jewish girl with the innocent blue eyes finally gave me the freedom to say, "To hell with Hitler."

24

Michaela

We were strangers before we became family. I was wrong about Blaze, and he was wrong about himself. Naomi was our responsibility. We had to get her to Switzerland. We'd been on the road for eight days, only two more to go.

If we survived this long, we could survive the next forty-eight hours, couldn't we?

The boy had become another tragedy of war. I blamed myself for what happened. If only I was one second faster. Naomi told me if I kept it up, I'd go crazy. She said I couldn't save everyone, but I had already saved her. Those words were enough to make me smile.

When the war started, I thought I would never be able to be happy again. Naomi had once again made the impossible come true.

We were back on the road by dawn. The day was clear and sunny; I felt nothing could go wrong. "When we get to Switzerland," Naomi said, "we're going to stay together, right?"

I spent so much time worrying about actually getting there, that I didn't even begin to think about what we'd do once we got there.

"I thought you had family there?" Blaze replied. She didn't have to say anything for me to know what she meant. Naomi had relatives in Switzerland, but she didn't know them.

"We're staying together," I said. I was certain we would, and we would've... if it weren't for what happened next.

25

Naomi

Soldiers surrounded us. They came from nowhere. My heart dropped. I looked to Blaze to find reassurance, but he seemed just as terrified as I was.

"My name is Blaze Weber," his voice was confident. "I am a Nazi soldier. I'm escorting these two lovely ladies to Switzerland on special orders from Hitler himself." Why had he just said that? We had no papers to prove that statement, and if they found out he wasn't telling the truth, they'd kill us. I couldn't save Chrissy, but I could save them.

"No," I began. "That's not the truth." Michaela and Blaze looked at me with concerned eyes. I knew those looks. It was the same I'd given Chrissy when she saved me. "I forced them to aid me to Switzerland. I told them if they didn't take me there I'd kill their families and then I'd kill them. I'm Jewish. I couldn't stay here."

The soldiers twitched when I said I was Jewish, like it was a terrible sin.

"Papers," one of them said to Blaze and Michaela. They handed over their documents reluctantly. "They're clear," he eventually said. I let out a sigh. I really didn't think that would work. The soldiers didn't say anything to me; one of them grabbed my hair and started yanking me towards the truck.

"Wait!" I hollered. "Let me say goodbye!" I pleaded. The soldier let go of my hair and grabbed my neck. He pulled my face close to his and whispered, "five minutes." He let go of me and pushed me towards my group. There was a smirk on his face, like he had just done some amazing act of kindness worthy of a medal.

Michaela was crying hard when I got to her, and Blaze pulled me in for a hug. "I'm sorry it took me so long," he cried.

I didn't know someone like him was capable of crying. I released myself from him and looked at both of them. It would be the last time I'd ever see them; I wanted a good look. I wanted to remember.

"You both saved me," I said. "Now let me save you." Michaela shook her head and hugged me tightly. Blaze wrapped his arms around us. It was one of the saddest moments I had ever experienced.

"That's enough," the soldier yelled. I heard him walking towards us to pull me away again, so I let go of my friends.

"Survive," I whispered. He yanked me away.

Escaping the Storm

26

Blaze

She said we had saved her; the opposite was true. Naomi had saved me in every way a person can be saved. She gave me my humanity back. She gave me my freedom. She gave me my hope. She gave me the honor of knowing her.

I held Michaela close to me as they dragged our friend away. Despite everything that was going on, Naomi still had the same look on her face; she was still the young

Jewish girl with the innocent blue eyes. That would be the last time I'd ever see her.

27

Michaela

I couldn't save Abbey. I couldn't save the boy. I couldn't save Naomi. Blaze held me as they dragged her away. I hid my face in his coat and cried; I cried until there were no tears left. The sound of the truck driving away would remain in my head forever. I had no picture of Naomi, but I would never forget what she looked like, what she sounded like, or what she'd done for me. I couldn't forget my savior.

Escaping the Storm

28

Blaze

It would be six years before I found out what happened to Naomi, and the answer would arrive in my mailbox. I received the letter two days ago, but the truth scared me and I didn't want to lose the last hope of her survival I had left.

Still, though, I needed to know. I opened the letter.

My dearest Blaze,

It's been two years since I last saw you. I know the truth of what happened that day haunts you like it does me.

I wanted you to know that I finally received the answers through an unlikely source. As you know, I fled to America after you left for Switzerland when the war ended. I've lived here for two years, but it wasn't until just recently that I found my best friend. I found Abbey.

She and her mother are alive and doing well. It is a miracle, really. I told her what you did for me, and I do want you to know she doesn't blame you for what happened to her, and neither do I.

Abbey said Naomi was sent to Auschwitz with her. From there, they were placed into intense labor, but Naomi kept the hope present. She often gave the little food she had to others, and was a mother figure for many young children.

Sixty million people perished during the war. Our Naomi was one of them. She died during December of 1944, though the specific date is unknown. Abbey said the young soldiers would often give her rations. It seems even the most evil of evils were drawn in by Naomi's light.

Her kindness was her doom. I met a few children who are now alive and free because of what Naomi did for them. Our Naomi remains a savior even in her death. She saved hundreds of lives in two years, more than anyone will ever do in a lifetime. She is buried in the camp among many others.

I haven't been there, but I hope to travel back to Germany and visit her soon. As for now, she is safe. She is free. She is loved.

-Michaela

About The Author

Katrina Wong is a 10th grade high school student in Virginia. She enjoys reading novels set in World War 2 and was inspired to write a short story about what life might have been like for a teenager during that time.

Katrina plans to major in English and elementary education when she starts college. This is her first published work of fiction.

Escaping the Storm

About The Publisher

Story Shares is a nonprofit focused on supporting the millions of teens and adults who struggle with reading by creating a new shelf in the library specifically for them. The ever-growing collection features content that is compelling and culturally relevant for teens and adults, yet still readable at a range of lower reading levels.

Story Shares generates content by engaging deeply with writers, bringing together a community to create this new kind of book. With more intriguing and approachable stories to choose from, the teens and adults who have fallen behind are improving their skills and beginning to discover the joy of reading. For more information, visit storyshares.org.

Easy to Read. Hard to Put Down.

Escaping the Storm

www.ingramcontent.com/pod-product-compliance
Lightning Source LLC
Chambersburg PA
CBHW051310170626
46809CB00004B/1839